GRANITE SHORES

And other Stories from Tibbitts Hill

C.J. Goodin

Tales from Tibbitts Hill

Imprint: Independently published

GRANITE SHORES AND OTHER STORIES FROM TIBBITTS HILL

and

TALES FROM TIBBITTS HILL

For permissions contact: obsidianringbusiness@gmail.com

ISBN: 979-8-218-06771-7

Cover Design by C.J. Goodin

Cover art by Lady Sara Richard

www.SaraRichard.com

Contents

Introduction

Cheers to broken dreams, the 'what ifs,' and what scares us.

Granite Shores is an homage to the cold dark world that forged the writer that I would one day become. Growing up influenced by Stephen King and LeVar Burton, I found my passion for storytelling once I started to mirror the events of my life into my own stories.

A special thank you to members of the #WritingCommunity: Natasha Link, Natalie Demoss, Michael Westmoreland, William Thomas Brumley, Krystal Sanders, Caitlyn Lasater, Tori Goggin, C.E. Wallace, and Kimberly Greer

Dedicated to my beautiful family

+

King

Lovecraft

Poe

Bierce

Chambers

Forgotten terrors beneath the waves

Drag lost souls to early graves

Where madness lingers and lovers mourn

But stranger still are these granite shores

<u>Granite Shores</u>

2022
Lunging Island, Isles of Shoals, NH

"Home sweet home," Carroll Deering mused as she sailed across the frigid waters toward Lunging Island.

It had been over fifteen years since Carroll left the cold New England coast to live with family in Virginia, and later started a career with the FBI. She never looked back to her tiny island village, but that was before she heard of her mother's illness, compelling her to return. Carroll bid her wife farewell and headed back home to that dreaded island.

The island was once a landing for seasonal fishermen from the colonies before eventually being bought by the wealthy Sampsons of Tibbitts Hill. Some believed God's whispers guided men to the island of jagged stone. Others say sirens. Either way, it was Reverend Sampson who governed the Island.

Carroll never felt comfortable in her town, or maybe the town never felt comfortable with her. Her mixed heritage alienated her from the community. She didn't make many friends. She was a reminder of her daddy, the outsider, who was unwelcome on the island and who died in a church fire when she was very young.

Rex Paxton, an acquaintance from her childhood, ferried her across the dark waters to the little village on this Tamberlane Supply boat. Hard to get to, even harder to breathe in. It had a lot of gossip and even more preaching. It's hard to keep a secret in a town of only two hundred, but which was secret was never discussed.

As Rex's boat arrived at Lunging, the pier looked the same as it ever did, greyed and worn. Passing people she had known from years before just glared at her arrival. As Rex tied the boat line to the dock, a woman in a dark gray dress approached, staring at Carroll.

"Well, if that isn't our little Carroll," the woman remarked as Carroll stepped onto the rickety beams of the pier.

"Hello, Ms. Appledore," Carroll greeted.

"My, don't you just look...," Ms. Appledore began. She smiled at Carroll's jeans and black tee shirt. "Bless your heart. Come with me, and we'll get you something warm to drink. It's quite cool out this evening."

"Yes, ma'am. Colder than a cadaver taken with the tide," Rex interjected.

"Take her bag to the *Jezebel Spirit* now," Ms. Appledore demanded with a scowl toward Rex. Ms. Appledore was a peculiar woman who offered Carroll her first job, working at the *Jezebel Spirit Inn*. The only traveler accommodation on the island. There was an odd sense of kindness to Ms. Appledore that the rest of the island did not share. Carroll had all but forgotten the *Jezebel Spirit Inn*. After years of nasty storms, she was surprised it still stood.

Once Rex was out of earshot, Ms. Appledore remarked to Carroll, "It has been a while since you have been home. Since you've chosen to neglect the island, many here aren't pleased about your return."

Carroll kept her eyes on the shoreside road as they walked past gawking townsfolk. The only woman with a cheerful demeanor hastily approached Carroll and Ms. Appledore from across the street. She wore a long light blue dress and a curious gold medallion that bounced off her ample chest.

At that moment, the air seemed to turn colder as a strong wind rolled off the coast.

"Here comes someone you could not have forgotten," Ms. Appledore said in almost a whisper before proclaiming toward the approaching woman. "Oh, Mrs. Sampson! Look who I found just washing up on our shores!"

"Oh, hello there, darlings!" replied the Reverend's wife.

A central family in the isles, the Sampsons were wealthy from generations of investors from Tibbitts Hill. Reverend Sampson became the only preacher in town after a fire burnt down Carroll's father's church with him in it. People on the island had agreed one church was enough for the island anyways.

"Our little Ms. Deering. Well, aren't you full grown? Hmmm, you used to be always so nervous all the time—just a long-tailed cat in a room full of rockers. I have always loved your color. Like useful leather. Useful, useful leather." Mrs. Sampson pulled the bewildered Carroll in for a quick hug. As she did so, she reached and touched Carroll's hair, remarking with a big smile that it, "feels like fresh wool."

Carroll couldn't only reply with anything but a hateful stare as she pushed back from the embrace.

"When did she arrive?" Mrs. Sampson asked, ignoring Carroll's expression.

"Rex just brought her in," Ms. Appledore replied.

"Oh, that ol' death trap? He still fancies you, you know? You used to be such a pretty little thing back then."

"I'm only here to visit my sick mother," Carroll huffed.

"Ha-ha, oh, Ms. Deering, aren't you just a small dark cloud on an otherwise sunny day! You're back, and we have you now. You will join us tonight for the revival, won't you?"

Before Carroll could reply, Ms. Appledore interjected, "I will be taking her to the *Jezebel Spirit* to rest first."

"This is all wonderful, but I would like to see my mother before it gets too dark," Carroll remarked to Mrs. Sampson.

"Oh, child, so quick about your business. These granite shores have you again. Here you will be a part of the great awakening," Mrs. Sampson said with a large malicious smile. Ms. Appledore tugged on Carroll's sleeve to lead her further down the road. They weren't a few feet away before Mrs. Sampson added, "and you still have your father's eyes."

Carroll kept quiet and followed Ms. Appledore away from Mrs. Sampson. Who now merely smiled and waved after them.

The main street was getting dark as the sun set, leaving only the dim street lanterns to light the twilight world around her.

The *Jezebel Spirit Inn* looked as she remembered. Three stories of peeling white paint with blue trimming. Carroll's bag lay by the entrance, to which Ms. Appledore remarked, "I see Rex couldn't be bothered to bring your luggage to your room."

Carroll was escorted inside and up to her room, and she saw it hadn't changed either. Musk and the scent of the harbor filled the room adorned with worn yellow wallpaper and a picture of a B-17 bomber. Ms. Appledore's grandfather's "*Jezebel Spirit*," of the Inn's namesake, hung as the lone decoration on the wall.

Ms. Appledore opened Carroll's bag on the bed and held up a firearm ammunition magazine. "You really believe you'll need this?"

"You never know," Carroll grimly said as she took the ammo magazine back.

Ms. Appledore smirked in return, "Come down when you're ready. I'll have supper for you."

"I'm not hungry. Thank you for your hospitality, but I need to see my mother. The rev..."

"It's not polite to refuse a home-cooked meal," Ms. Appledore implored, then turned and walked out of the room and down the steps. Carroll sighed and followed after placing the spare magazine back in her bag.

Her meal was quiet—chowder with a warm wedge of cornbread on the side. The food was hot, but it didn't change the chill in the air.

"Marie, your mother, is not well child. A few of us visit her, but she is not welcoming. She has been having strange visions of black stars and being chained to the shore. She dreams of Carcosa."

"I'm just here to see my mother. Make sure she's alright; then I'm leaving."

"I'm trying to tell you she's not alright."

Carroll finished her bowl and excused herself. Ms. Appledore inquired, "You remember where you are going, child? It's been an awful long time since you've been here. Maybe I should show you the way?"

"I'll manage just fine, thank you. This place doesn't change," Carroll remarked. Ms. Appledore could only nod in reply and closed the door behind Carroll as she walked out onto the street.

She headed towards her mother's house, alone on the north part of the island, off a dirt road resting on the shoreline.

Once far from downtown, she could see the reverend's church in the distance on the island's largest hill adjacent to the sea. She stopped momentarily to look at the lonely chapel overlooking the cold waves as a single candle flickered in a window.

"*The Blood of the Blessed Land*, she's special. Isn't she?" Said a deep voice behind her. "Guiding all that come to her for safe harbor like a lighthouse in a storm with her sacred word."

Carroll turned to see Reverend Sampson standing with an umbrella in his hand. His medallion shined somehow, even in the dark. How he held himself was not normal for a man of faith. Too confident and too forward. And the way he spoke was often broken and disjoined, difficult for Carroll to follow.

"That hill once had monks who forged dark metals into strange forms, quenching them in the unforgiving sea. It's going to rain soon," he said with a smile. Almost as if by command, it began to sprinkle. "Come with me, child. I heard you want to see your mother, and you're not wearing your talisman. I thought I would join you."

He leaned into Carroll, placing her under his umbrella as they walked silently down the long dirt road as the rain started to grow. She could hardly see anything in the dark other than the reverend's eyes peering down at her. Carroll held a hand on her concealed weapon, uneasy in his presence.

"Well, this is awfully kind of you, but I believe I know the rest of the way."

"I'm sure you do, but I'm here to give you spiritual guidance, Carroll. You've been gone an awfully long time and..."

"Reverend, I'm just here to see my mother. I won't even be here long. I'm leaving tomorrow."

"Well, your mother is... not well. I'm afraid she's been needing some help. Eating, cleaning, and bathing. She's all but let your home fall apart."

Carroll did not reply and kept quiet for the remainder of their walk.

As soon as they arrived at her mother's home, the reverend put away his umbrella. The rain immediately stopped falling. Trying not to fixate on the strange occurrence, Carroll knocked on the door. The silence made Carroll even more alert. Reverend Sampson turned the knob and walked in. Inside, empty bottles, little black books, and moldy food littered the floor.

Reverend Sampson remarked, "She'll be down the stairs out back. I will go make some tea."

Carroll exited through the back door to see a lone figure standing ankle-deep in the frigid sea.

The faint glimmer from the windows scarcely offered any light on her mother, Marie. She stood soaking wet in her nightgown, indifferent to the waves around her.

"Momma?" Carroll said and ran to her mother's side in the water, "Momma, are you alright?"

With closed eyes, her mother opened her arms wide to the sea and proudly proclaimed, "My eyes have seen the king in his beauty and his land that is very far off."

"Momma?" Carroll said, shaking her shoulders.

"He was a nice boy. He grew up so strong. Marie, he called me, Marie," Marie stammered out.

"Let's get you inside, mom. You're going to catch a cold out here all wet."

"He would hold me! His arms! So strong I couldn't even move to save you!" Marie shouted as she sat down in the water, crying into her knees.

"Momma, did the reverend do something to you? What happened?"

Carroll was cautious as she held her mother. Only her mother's head turned, now smiling but with her eyes still closed. Her mother handed her a little black book. Confused, Carroll opened it only to see random drawings and incomprehensible words, then stuffed it in her pocket.

Marie whispered, "Leave this place, save the words."

Carroll could only shake her head in confusion.

Marie just kept nodding and repeating, "Leave this place. Leave this place."

Carroll could only watch in dismay as her mother burst into spontaneous laughter.

"You know your daddy loved to give sermons. He thought he…." She paused and began to tip as if she were about to fall asleep. Then, in a hypnotized tone, Marie said, "I remember the gentle warm breeze that night as the flames blew past the burning church. It purified him and kept the Nagorath at bay. We did what the reverend needed us to do. He needed to be awakened."

"Mom, let's get you back inside, and we can talk about this. I can get you off this island."

"NO!" Marie exclaimed. She scooped up handfuls of rocks from the beach and threw them blindly into the crashing waves around her before collapsing in the water, laughing and shouting, "It's coming! It's coming again!"

All Carroll could do was stand and watch, confused and heartbroken about her mother's condition.

"The king has given me the gospel! He will rule with an iron rod, and the leaders of armies will be cast into a lake of fire. God has lost count of our horrors and has long since not cared." Carroll's mother opened her eyes to reveal two empty sockets where her eyes should've been. Horrified, Carroll moved back from her mother, who now gleefully played in the water, splashing as a child would. Eyeless in the crashing waves.

Carroll was startled when she turned to see Reverend Sampson on the balcony looking down at the beach. Carroll drew her pistol and aimed it at the reverend.

He calmly walked down the stairs to the shore, walking past Carroll to her mother. Marie reached her arms up to the preacher and held to him as she cried. His words seemed to comfort her, "Oh Marie, your eyes have seen a land very far off."

Reverend Sampson turned a lingering gaze to Carroll with a soft smile, "I'm having a revival tonight, Carroll. We require a great awakening within you, for it comes tonight."

Figure 1.

The reverend reached out for Carroll's hand, and his eyes turned black.

Carroll kept her aim on Reverend Sampson and began taking steps back, then ran up the staircase and back through the house. She sprinted down the road in almost pure darkness as the rain started to pick up again.

When she arrived at the *Jezebel Spirit,* she ran up to her room and slammed the door behind her.

Carroll was closing her bag to leave when she heard someone walk up the old creaking wooden stairs and towards her door. The groaning wood only intensified as the steps drew nearer to Carroll's room. Carroll aimed her pistol chest high at the entrance to the hallway. Several knocks came along with Ms. Appledore's voice, "I've prepared some tea. Would you care to join me?"

Carroll brought her gun down to her lap and spoke as calmly as possible, "No, thank you. I'm just going to get in some early rest for tomorrow."

"Well, Ms. Deering. If you should need anything, I will be downstairs."

"Thank you, Ms. Appledore, and goodnight."

"Goodnight."

Carroll could hear Ms. Appledore go back down the stairs to the first floor. She sat on the edge of the bed, waiting until she could no longer hear steps, then exited through her window without making a sound. She left the inn and headed towards the pier, hoping to find Rex's boat.

As she briskly walked down the street in the now heavy rain, Carroll began to see faces moving after her. Their eye watched her more intently as she walked. The size of the crowds grew, torches started being lit, and the faces began to multiply. Carroll quickened her pace as the street lamps' light started to die, leaving her in the dark. The island turned utterly black except for the flames and the faces that carried them.

Just as she turned the corner to the pier, she noticed Rex Paxton standing beside his Tamberlane boat on the dock.

"Rex!" Carroll shouted. Rex looked startled at Carroll as she speedily approached him, "We have to leave here now!"

"Carroll, I can't..."

More and more townsfolk began approaching the docks with lit torches.

Carroll took out her pistol and aimed it at him, "We are leaving now!"

"I can't do that."

Voices began to chant as the faces encroached on Carroll, "Purify. Purify. Purify."

"I'm commandeering your vehicle!" Carroll began to shiver in the pelting rain. Boards on the docks started to buckle from the weight of the townsfolk.

Rex stepped toward Carroll once, and she fired two rounds into his chest. Without hesitation, she jumped into the boat and unhitched the line from the dock. She started the engine and sped off back across the dark waters toward the shores of Rye under the cover of stars.

Carroll arrived on the mainland an hour later and took the first flight back to Virginia. Once she arrived, she was immediately called to her superior's office.

"Didn't you just come from Lunging Island?"

Carroll nodded in his direction. "There's something you need to see."

As Carroll stepped towards his desk, local news coverage from the isles played on his monitor:

> "A Tamberlane Supply boat registered to Lunging Island native Rex Payton was washed up on Rye Beach. When authorities attempted to contact the small village, they found no one alive on the island. State and local law enforcement have yet to find a single living person in their six-hour search. Only two deceased persons; Rex Payton, the leasee of the boat, reportedly shot twice, and a currently unidentified older woman outside the *Jezebel Spirit Inn*, who may have been burned alive. We will report with updates on this story as we get them. This is Scarlet O'Brian, Channel 4 News."

Her supervisor looked up from his seat at Carroll, "What can you tell me about this place?"

"Only to never go there."

Gas Station Night Shift Phone Calls

Summer 1997
Weare, NH

The small gas station off the turnpike sat as it always had. Shelves half empty.

Working at a gas station is never anyone's dream job. However, Alexis didn't mind it when she was alone. She only hated the job when Cecil was around to talk at her. Ever since he became store manager of the Econo-Gas gas station by his dad, Cecil had become even less bearable. Over the past several months, he had jockeyed the schedule so that Zoe worked the early mornings, leaving Alexis with the night shift.

 "Soon, we'll be the best gas station in Weare, New Hampshire!" Cecil declared as he finished putting up a tacky paper banner to celebrate the new management. He cooled himself with the counter fan as he admired his work.

"More like nowhere, New Hampshire," Alexis said under her breath about the small rural New England village.

Whenever Cecil got into one of his rants, she could usually tune him out, but Cecil seemed particularly obsessive about improving the store this evening. He must've heard about the Tamberlane Supply bid for an Econo Gas in Tibbitt's Hill. His constant effort to try and sell the forsaken gas station always got under Alexia's skin, as she would likely lose her job.

The station had struggled long before Cecil took over management. Something he tried to remedy with every other idea from a recent small business seminar he attended. He added trucker hats, 'Live Free or Die' fridge magnets, and Weare-wolf plushie dolls for the tourists that never drove through.

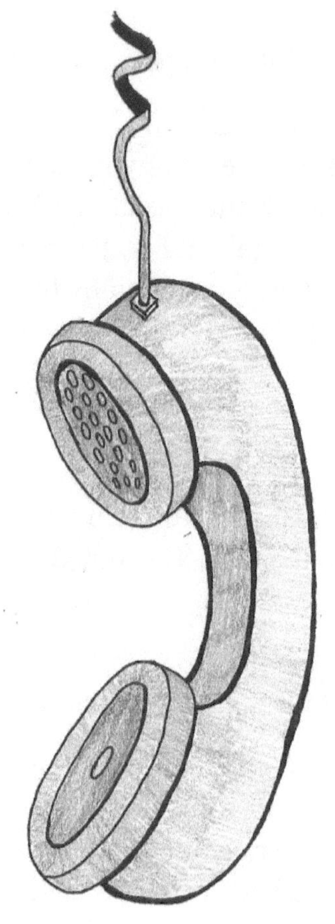

Figure 2.

"You should've seen it. The seminar had a big ol' chart with tons of good ideas on it. Sometimes you have to cut things off to make room for new stuff. That's why I cut back on some stuff to get some tourist stuff. Tourists love buying dumb things," Cecil scoffed as he stared proudly at the tall rack by the counter. "Also, the seminar said that we could make ten percent more money by being friendly on the phone. Imagine that? We'll be even better than Tasia Gas. You'll see. So just stick to a customer service script I had Zoe make."

Cecil grabbed his keys from the counter and started for the door, reminding Alexis, "Oh, and we are out of gas canisters and the bathroom toilet paper. A roll is only fifty cents for employees if you need to go. I forgot to place an order with Tamberlane Supply. Leave a note for Zoe to order those tomorrow morning. Oh, and the trash by the back door needs to be taken out."

"Yup, got it," Alexis remarked, barely paying attention as she read from a little black book.

Cecil just sighed at her response, put on an Econo Gas trucker's hat, and exited the station toward his yellow truck.

The moment Cecil left, the phone began to ring.

Brrring, Brrring

Alexis knew that if she ignored it, the ringing would eventually stop, just as any other shift.

A car horn blared in the parking lot. Alexis looked up from her book and saw Cecil motioning with an arm out the truck window for Alexis to pick up the receiver.

She rolled her eyes, put down her book, and answered the phone.

"Hello?" Alexis greeted, making direct eye contact with Cecil.

"What do you mean 'hello?' You need to read off the card," Cecil reprimanded, then waved his phone in the air. Alexis had forgotten about Cecil's promotion bonus from his dad. A dumb new cellular phone.

"I'll be making sure you answer the phone correctly. If you don't pick up, I'm gonna need to let you go."

Alexis knew that few places besides gas stations gave high school dropouts a chance. She just nodded with frustration, conceding with a heavy sigh.

"Good. So can you read it off for me?"

Alexis replied with a mock receptionist tone, "Thank you for calling Econo Gas, located right off route 114. How can I help?"

"We can't be strangers. It's 'My name is Alexis. How may I help you?' Just stick to the card. You're gonna do great!" Cecil pressed a button on his cellular phone to hang up, reversed his truck, and drove off.

Alexis slammed the phone down and muffled a scream into a Weare-wolf plushie before shoving it back on the rack.

It wasn't five minutes later that the phone rang again.

Brrring, Brrring

Alexis took a deep breath and picked up the phone, figuring it was Cecil testing her again.

"Thank you for calling Econo Gas, located right off route 114. My name is Alexis. How may I help you?"

Heavy Breathing "Yes, hello?" The stranger asked.

"Hello? Cecil?" Alexis asked back, confused by the tone and the breathing. The voice sounded horse and laborious, unlike Cecil's.

"Oh, thank god. Do you guys sell gas cans?"

"Sorry, we are out," Alexis said, remembering what Cecil mentioned.

"Please. I've run out of gas, and I've walked a long way. I need one."

"Sorry, you'll need to try Tasia Gas further in town," Alexis rolled her eyes and started to play with the phone cord twisting it around her fingers.

"Please, ma'am, I need a gas can," The stranger begged.

"I already told you. I'm sorry, but we are out," Alexis said with irritation.

"Could you check again?"

Frustrated, Alexis put the phone down on the counter. She walked around the plushie rack to look at the empty shelf where gas canisters once sat and then back to the phone.

With a reluctant begrudging tone, Alexis confirmed, "Just double-checked. Nothing."

"Please, ma'am, I need a gas can." The stranger begged again.

"Sorry, man. We're out. Good luck at Tasia Gas."

Alexis hung up the phone. Annoyed, Alexis hoped it would be the last call of the night. She opened her book again to continue to read.

Brrring, Brrring

Alexis sighed and debated whether or not just to let it ring.

Brrring, Brrring

She knew she couldn't listen to it all night and answered the call.

"Thank you for calling Econo Gas. My name is Alexis. How can I help you?"

Heavy Breathing "Yes, hello?" Asked the stranger.

"Cecil, is this you?" Asked Alexis.

"Oh, thank god. Do you guys sell gas cans?" The stranger asked. Alexis knew it was the same man who had just called.

"Sorry, I already told you. We are out. Try calling Tasia Gas. They're still open."

"Please, ma'am. I need a gas can." The stranger's voice sounded very raspy.

"Sir, I'm going to let you go. Good luck trying to find it." Alexis started to get a little nervous from his shift in voice.

"Wait, please!" Cried the stranger.

Alexis threw down the phone, lightly panting as she did.

    Brrring, Brrring

    Brrring, Brrring

Alexis closed her eyes in frustration and answered the call.

"Hello?"

"Oh, thank god. Do you guys sell gas cans?" Asked the stranger.

Alexis hung up the phone.

    Brrring, Brrring

"Stop calling here!" Alexis cried as she picked up the receiver.

"Oh, thank god. Do you guys sell gas cans?" Asked the stranger.

"For the last time, no! We don't have any!" Alexis yelled into the phone.

"Please, ma'am. I need a gas can," begged the stranger.

Alexis slammed down the receiver, gritting her teeth in anger. She struck the phone several more times, then ripped the phone line from the wall.

    Brrrii-

Alexis turned the counter fan to cool herself down. She couldn't understand what was going on.

After an hour passed, Cecil's yellow truck drove back by. Alexis knew he'd call again, and this was likely him just taking the joke too far. She recomposed herself and reconnected the phone to the wall.

Immediately the ringing continued.

> *-iiinng, Brrring*

> *Brrring, Brrring*

Alexis picked up the receiver.

"Hello?"

"Oh, thank god. Do you guys sell gas cans?" Asked the stranger.

"No," Alexis said, her voice filled with frustration.

"Please, ma'am. I need a gas can."

"Alright. Come here and see for yourself that I have no gas canisters."

"This is a long walk, and I'm alone now." *thud*

"What was that?" Alexis asked the stranger.

"What was what?" The stranger replied.

"There was a thud sound."

"Walking alone is kinda scary. I hope you don't mind if I stay on the line with you while I walk?" The stranger shifted to an almost happy tone that unsettled Alexis deeply.

"Um, no. I'll see you when I see you."

Alexis hung up the phone.

> *Brrring, Brrring*

Alexis picked the phone back up.

"Stop calling and just walk here."

"Oh, thank god. Do you guys sell gas cans?" Asked the stranger.

"I already said come here and see."

"This is a long walk, and I'm alone now." *thud*

"What was that sound again? You did it again." Alexis caught her voice starting to quiver.

"Walking alone is kinda scary. I hope you don't mind if I stay on the line with you while I walk?" The stranger's asked with a sense of desperation in his voice.

"Why?"

"Well. It's dark, and I'm… *grunt* alone now."

"What are you doing?" demanded Alexis.

"I'm walking toward you. I think I can see the lights."

"Fine, then, just come here. I'm hanging up now."

"Please don't," begged the stranger.

"If you can see it, you can just walk the rest of the way."

Alexis slammed down the phone again.

 Brrring, Brrring

Alexis's face was filled with rage as she picked up the phone and shouted, "What the hell is the matter with you? If you keep calling, then… then I'll call the police."

"Oh, thank god. Do you guys sell gas cans?" Asked the stranger.

"Why do you keep repeating yourself?" Alexis felt crushed by the stranger's indifference to her threat.

"This is a long walk, and I'm alone now." *thud*

Abrasively confused, Alexis leaned forward over the counter and stretched the coiled phone cord to look further out the front windows. She pulled as far as she could and frantically looked down the road to see if she could see the strange man walking.

"Walking alone is kinda scary. I hope you don't mind if I stay on the line with you while I walk?" Asked the stranger.

"That's fine," Alexis reluctantly replied, her eyes watering from anxiety. Unsure of what to do.

"It's dark, and I'm *grunt* alone now," the stranger forced out

 Alexi's eyes darted around, peering out the windows as far as she could to try and see the approaching stranger.

"I'm walking to you. I can see the lights right there," the stranger with a weird rising optimism in his voice.

Alexis could no longer take it. She dropped the phone on the counter, backed away, and breathed deeply. She tried to control her growing anxiety that was turning into a gripping fear.

"Ma'am, are you there? Please tell me if you can hear me," begged the stranger with concern in his voice.

Alexis closed her eyes and continued taking deep breaths, ignoring the stranger speaking through the phone. Until the disconnect tone rang, followed by the off-hook tone alert. Its sound was just as piercing as the ringing. She could only endure it momentarily before slamming the receiver back on the phone mound.

 Brrring, Brrring

 Brrring, Brrring

She gathered herself as she leaned on the counter, took one last deep breath, and then picked up the phone.

"Hello?" She said with caution.

"Oh, thank god. Do you guys sell gas cans?" Asked the stranger.

"Yes," Alexis lied.

"This is a long walk, and I'm alone now." *thud*

"You can talk if you want," Alexis sniffled back tears.

"Thank you. Walking alone is kinda scary. It's dark, and I'm *grunt* alone now."

Alexis gave a nervous laugh at the idea of this stranger being scared. Her anxiety made her hands tremble, and her legs felt like jelly. Her eyes began to tear up in terror as only the stranger's grunts and movements could be heard over the phone.

"Hello?" The stranger asked.

"I'm still here," Alexis reluctantly replied, wiping her moist eyes.

"I'm walking toward you. I can see the lights right there."

Alexis sniffled with anticipation with her glossed-over eyes, still looking out of the gas station's windows to see anyone walking from either direction.

"Are you still there? Please tell me if you can hear me," begged the stranger with concern in his voice.

"I'm here," Alexis reassured, gripping the receiver tightly.

"Good. Good." The stranger spoke with such a sigh of relief. He let out an exhausted but sexually gratified moan just before asking, "Could you do me a big favor and unlock the dumpster out back? I- *grunt* I need to throw out some trash I brought with me."

A tear rolled down Alexis's cheek as she stood silently at the counter.

"Are you there?" Asked the stranger.

Distraught but determined, Alexis whispered through gritted teeth, "Yes, I'm still here."

"What's your name?" The stranger asked with an almost sensual tone.

"Alexis," she sputtered out, only to be met with heavy breathing.

Suddenly violent hammering on the back door rattled its hinges. The forceful battering caused Alexis to scream and drop the phone on the counter.

"Alexis, open the door!" Commanded the stranger sternly over the phone.

Although his voice was urgent, it was much calmer than the striking of the back door. Each bang sounded like it could be its last. The strikes were getting louder and faster as the stranger on the phone kept demanding that Alexis unlock the back door.

"Alexis, open the door! Alexis, open the door! Alexis, open the door!"

The stranger repeated on the phone, sounding more feral and maniacal each time. She couldn't listen to the stranger anymore and slammed down the phone.

The hammering on the door immediately stopped, and the phone began to ring again.

Brrring, Brrring

Brrring, Brrring

Brrring, Brrring

Brrring, Brrring

Brrring, Brrring

"Thank you for calling Econo Gas," Alexis muttered in terror.

"Oh, thank god. Do you guys sell gas cans?" Asked the stranger.

An Old Sailor's Tale to a Young Sailor

1876
Atlantic Ocean
The Niflheim

A young sailor looked to the edge of the world from the bow, right where the sky meets the sea, and saw a green light flash in the evening's descending darkness. He stared in disbelief. Seeing what he had only heard about in stories.

"Some say that light are souls, returning from the land of the dead, what our ancestors called *Niflheim*. Our ship's namesake. But I believe it's a sign you should get back to swabbing the deck. If you have time to stand around looking at lights, you have time to clean. Skippers orders," the old sailor hissed, throwing the young sailor a mop. The young sailor begrudgingly fetched a pail.

The old sailor sat back on a strapped barrel and lit up his pipe as the young sailor mopped. After a puff of smoke, the old sailor continued to speak, "I'll have you know we always leave for the Isles at dark so that we will have morning's first light in the returning trip. Whoever it is that makes it back, that is."

The young sailor was caught off guard and tripped over his pail, becoming irritated. "Aren't we about to wade into a storm? And you're sure this can't wait?"

The old sailor ignored the question. "You know, I remember my first supply delivery; I also saw the green flash. I was a young lad around your age, a few of the crew told me the green light was death, coming from the waters, preparing to drag lost sailors into a watery grave. A farewell to anyone unfit to be on these seas. But what I remember most that night was the eerie black waters and what they failed to hide…." The old sailor trailed off and puffed on his pipe.

Figure 3.

The young sailor picked up the pail and continued to swab the deck. The boat rocked as the swell of the sea began to rise. A cool salty mist in the air from the waves slapping the ship's side sprayed across the young sailor's face. As he wiped his face, he started to hear whistling. The young sailor turned to see the old sailor with closed eyes whistling out *The Dying soldier*.

"I don't believe in the old sea myths," the young sailor said. He tried to ignore the old sailor's whistling as he worked amid the growing waves.

Raindrops put out the old sailor's pipe embers, and the young sailor chuckled before a wave leaped over the edge and struck his face again.

It was becoming too dark to clean, and the young sailor cursed as he repeatedly tripped over the pail and fell to the deck. In frustration, the young sailor barked, "We can't see anything without the floodlights. Why aren't the lights on?"

The old sailor ignored the young sailor's question and spoke as he tried to relight his pipe, "Oh, of course, I didn't believe in the old sea myths back then, either. Just the murmurings of drunken sailors just trying to scare a boot. Talk of the likes of merfolk, leviathans, and all else in these dark waters."

A distant but thunderous roar echoed around them in the dark sea. It was a surreal endless black void. Only the dim glow of the storm, the cabin, and the flicker of the old sailor's lighter could be seen in the wonder of darkness. Without further hesitation, the young sailor ran to find the floodlight panel and turned them on in the last semblance of light. Only to see the light devoured by the void immediately around them.

While he dried his pipe, the old sailor spoke again, "That island is filled with monks. Deformed zealots of an unholy cult. They are to blame for the dense fog. Just breathing the island air for too long is said to drive a man mad. A living storm looms over them isles. The further the boat sailed, the more it felt like… like we were inside something. Like a churning, swollen belly."

The old sailor tried again to light his pipe. The lighter flickered in the dancing rain, dying with every strike. The thunder roared, and the old sailor abandoned lighting his pipe, putting it aside in his pocket. He got off his barrel and approached the young sailor, "Ashore, shadows and time bend. I've seen chanting priests who didn't fear the dark and that mated with screeching sirens on jagged rocks. I saw beyond death at the center of the island."

The young sailor could not tell from which way the wind blew and found it hard to breathe on the rocking ship. The roar of the thunder was intensifying, and the wind brought him to his knees. The crushing black waters that lapped over the side felt his skin tare with its icy touch.

The old sailor shouted over the thunder, "In these waters, this ship *Niflheim* is the only refuge from the maddening sea and from what crawls from its deeps. The green light was a sign that you should've turned back. What lurks beneath the sea is coming for your soul, boy, and it doesn't matter if you believe in it or not! "

The wind flew passed the rocks, whistling in the air and growing into a cacophony as the ship grew closer to tall, dark stones jetting out from the water. The young sailor swore he heard screaming and laughter from figures leaping into the sea. When the young sailor peered over the edge to see where the creatures may have gone, he saw a sea of tentacles. Oily black writhing in the waves. He began to lean too far over the bow when the old sailor pulled him back. They struggled back across the deck into the bridge as the swells grew. The winds roared, and the waves battered the ship's sides.

The *Niflheim's* fog lights finally caught sight of the island's rotting dock through the stormy winds. The old sailor and the young sailor returned to the deck as they approached the pier. The rain lessened as they tied the ferry to the docks, the waves subsided, and the wailing of the storm was calmed.

The old sailor tossed two large bags to the young sailor and motioned him to bring the supplies ashore. As the young sailor hesitantly obliged, he stepped off the boat. Once his feet touched the island, hooded monks with pale white skin emerged from the fog. Silently they motioned the young sailor to follow them back into the dense dark vapors. The young sailor looked back at the old sailor leaning against the foremast, focused on relighting his pipe. He steeled his nerve and stepped into the fog.

The skipper stepped out from the bridge and leaned close to the old sailor, "You telling stories to nubs again, eh? Merfolk or leviathans?"

"Mad monks on the island," the old sailor answered, finally managing to relight his pipe.

The skipper chuckled, "Aye, that's a good tale."

<u>Pareidolia</u>

2003
Franconia, NH

"I saw a great face high in the mountain, but in time it fell away," the old man wrote along the edges of his little black book as he sat alone in his mountain cabin. "The world had changed so much since the faces arrived."

Faces. Arriving and dissipating. Expressionless. Appearing in water, food, fire, and dreams. Some vanished just as quickly as they appeared. Others would linger.

No one claimed to know where the faces came from or what they were. Some told the retired harbormaster they hadn't seen any, but the old man was sure everyone saw them. Rare at first, they steadily grew in size and number. Day and night, becoming madness itself.

It all began on a warm August night in the Rye harbor when the tide swept a derelict boat into the port. Once captured, the old harbormaster only found a small black book beside the helm. The first face appeared not long after he had flipped through its pages.

A strange pallid face, just floating in the harbor lights near its entrance. Not knowing what it was, the old harbormaster directed an approaching ship to turn. The boat struck a rock just under the water's surface, and the following collision killed two people on board. No one believed the harbormaster and forced him to turn his position over to his assistant. Who drowned a week later under mysterious circumstances.

The retired harbormaster began to see faces in clouds, on clothes, and even reflections in mirrors. He thought about speaking with the priest, but he knew the church would soon crumble under the madness the faces brought, bringing about the end of days. They could not help anyone now.

Reading from the black book was the only time the old man didn't see faces. The old harbormaster knew it would be insane to stay and hadn't heard of any by the mountain cabin he grew up in. He left with his wife without warning once the town barred him from the harbor.

But the faces found them. They lingered in shadows and walls. The old man swore he heard some of the faces speak. Their lips didn't move, but he could hear their taunts, dread, and cries just the same.

Little seemed to matter to his wife anymore. She only gritted her teeth whenever the old man tried to talk to her about the faces. He believed she was jealous of his book; maybe she had already gone mad. One night it was too much for his wife, and she left in the truck while he was asleep.

There was nowhere to escape the faces. Travel became impossible. His wife was a fool.

A face on the side of the mountain crumbled and fell, and the news became unbearable to watch.

Mania had settled in the old man once the faces started to look like people he knew.

Old friends and family. Those who didn't believe him and the useless priest. His deceiving wife and betraying assistant. The old man kept to the black book in the cabin as long as he could. Drawing in abstracts, and writing the words from the voices, over already filled-in pages.

Until one day, the old man of the mountain collapsed.

He awoke to an old melodic song that rested over the chaotic sound of the faces just outside the cabin door. The old man walked out of the cabin only to see his wife's face floating in the air and ran after her.

Figure 4.

For two days, he followed her face over rocks and through forests. Day and night. From the mountains to the shore. He followed her until her face shined over his old harbor and descended back into the fog on the horizon. The retired harbormaster climbed the derelict boat and waded out to sea after it.

<u>Bound on a Rock</u>

Awakened by a cruel, frigid wave, I found myself bound to a rock.

Immobile and imposed, I faced nothing but an endless dark ocean with my arms forcibly stretched out wide and tightly latched onto the boulder that jetted out of the shore. Only once I looked furthest to my left did I see a middle-aged man shackled like me on a large granite boulder of his own.

"What is this?" I asked the man as I tried to move my hands in the straps.

"We are attached to rocks," He replied.

"But why am I here?"

The man replied, "I don't know why I am here. I certainly don't know why you're here."

After a moment of contemplation, I realized I could not remember my name. I didn't know if I had a family or a home. All I knew was that I was chained to a rock and began crying.

I looked back at the man, who looked like he was crying as well, and asked, "How long have you been here?"

"I arrived just before you, after the woman on my right, and I'm telling you everything she told me."

"What?"

At that moment, a massive wave arrived and covered us both. When the surge subsided, I looked to my left and saw a woman chained and bound on a large rock as well.

I cried out, but she seemed delirious. She looked below and up before noticing me.

"What is this?" She demanded as she tried to move her hands in the straps.

"We are attached to rocks," I replied.

"But why am I here?"

I replied, "I don't know why I am here. I certainly don't know why you are here."

She began to cry. After a moment, she looked back at me, studying the tears trickling down my face.

"How long have you been here?"

"I arrived just before you, after the man on my right, and I'm telling you everything he told me."

"What?"

Another large wave crashed against us.

"Hey," cried the man from my left. I turned back to realize he had a short white beard that I must have missed before. "You need to listen to me. We don't have long."

"I know what you're going to say. The woman beside me is a little hysterical, but she might know something we don't."

"Stop. You need to listen to me. You're just doing what I'm doing," cried out the man.

"Hold on, let me get her again," and I turned back toward the woman. She looked focused to her right. Before I could speak, another mighty wave bashed the shoreside boulders.

"Hey," I cried back over at the woman. When she turned back toward me, her face looked aged. I realized we were getting older.

"You need to listen to me. We don't have much time," I said.

"I know what you're going to say. The woman beside me is a little hysterical, but she might know something we don't."

"Stop. You need to listen to me. You're just doing what I'm doing."

Figure 5.

"Hold on, let me get her again," and then she turned back to her right.

Before I could get another word out to her, another cold wave rushed against us. Its icy waters caused my skin to tear.

I turned back to my right, and now an old man with a long white scraggly beard was bound to the rock. Frail in the shackles. Seemingly too tired to speak.

"I believe I have it figured out. We are in a coil. What you say is what I'll say. Tell me what the woman to your right said," I frantically asked in desperation.

The old man gave a slow, sad smile and died. The waves crashed again, and the old man vanished from his shackles.

I was in pain, felt weak, and could feel my body give way to the rising tide. I looked back to the woman, who was noticeably older now.

"I believe I have it figured out. We are in a coil. What you say is what I'll say. Tell me what the man to your right said," she frantically asked in desperation.

I mustered what I could of a small smile and closed my eyes to the crack of a frigid wave washing over me.

Falcon Heights

When I was a little boy, I lived in a haunted house on Tibbitts Hill.

A real haunted house?

Obviously not. That's just a silly story I like to tell people.

It was just an old home. A nineteenth-century colonial built by a retired doctor on a hundred-acre former plantation on the outskirts of a tiny New England village. The house was buckled and worn, white paint peeled from its old wooden siding, and was guarded by two tall ascending rows of dark green hedges. The house had a big red front door that creaked and moaned, with the house's name was etched into a wooden plaque just above it:

Falcon Heights

Crackling floorboards and aching staircases sounded like as if every nail seemed ready to fall out. The house was fighting for survival in a world that no longer wanted it.

But, still, not a haunted house.

The spring on Tibbitts Hill brought pollen and bees to the top of the stone-walled dirt mound. Its woods were old but new. The former pine tree plantation, that once made masts for ships, had long since been left unattended and became a dark forest that was my backyard. Whose bark looked like an endless choir of faces, whistling with the passing wind. It was my pine tree cathedral, and eyes often stared at me, but always just out of sight.

The summer heat drove the insects to eat the rotting product from the abandoned vineyards. Overgrown grapes and apples grew wild and bitter without anyone tending to them. Vines had overtaken the double bench swing, and the cabin in the woods fell into disrepair.

Autumn's ever-encroaching darkness won a little more each day. The warm hues of red and yellow maple leaves turned brown and then black, and the sun would hide away. I knew the shadows would play tricks in the fall. I'd feel their smiles while I played. And as the air turned colder, the movement in the woods would grow.

What beauty was found in autumn was quickly choked by the frost of winter. The white death. Everything was stripped of its color, and the hillside was buried in heavy snow. Blizzards would screech in an agonizing horrid chorus, and whatever the winds didn't say, the groaning house would, as the old glass windows would rattle against the frigid wind. It was too easy to imagine a voice, something calling out, in the dark winter months.

Any cold winter night, I would lie in bed thinking of dark questions which no one wanted to answer. Like, why did the good doctor need the shackles in the basement? Were his days as a surgeon behind him, or did his desire for strange wisdom expand? Whose faces were those deep in the woods? And were their screams lost in the buffeting winds?

Who was it peering into my window from the edge of the woods? And why did it smile with such sad eyes? And why did it tell me to run? Was it him who walked in the attic at night? Was he the one who kept writing in the little black book I found?

No.

Figure 6.

It's just a silly little story I tell about the old house I grew up in.

Random Box™

Ding Dong

When I opened the door, I found a strange Random Box.

"I don't remember ordering one," I thought and put the Random Box and some junk mail on the kitchen table.

'Someone has sent you a *Random Box™*,' is all the inscription said. Not a single blemish on any side, and very light. I brought it to the kitchen counter, cut its thick tape, and opened it to find a small black book inside. After looking outside the box again for other clues as to who sent it, I put the rest of the junk mail in the opened box and walked to the living room to read my new little black book.

Later, my wife woke me from the couch and asked when I planned on opening the Random Box to see what was inside. Confused, I returned to the kitchen to find the Random Box sitting unopened beside the junk mail. I reopened the box and saw a little black book as before, unsure where I had placed my old one.

"Stress," I thought to myself. "I must just be misremembering."

Long after my wife was in bed, I took a break from reading the strange little book of odd writings for a late-night snack and found the box sitting entirely unopened on the kitchen counter.

"I know I've opened this," I thought, reexamining the box from every angle to confirm if it was indeed the same. I opened it again to find it still with the book. I collapsed the box and placed it next to the trash to throw it out the following morning.

Making it a point the moment I woke up to throw out the trash, to again find the box intact on the kitchen counter. Frustrated, I swiftly brought it to the outdoor recycling bin and threw it in.

To my annoyance, I found another box on my car's passenger seat when I started to leave for work. I threw it out the window before driving, only for it to frustrate me when the same box appeared again at my desk. I must've looked crazy, demanding answers from coworkers about who had given me the Random Box. I placed it under my desk and left for home, where I found another Random Box on the front porch, and I immediately threw it in the trash can. Only to be greeted by the same package again the following morning. I brought it to the neighbor's house, dropped it on their doorstep, and ran away.

I spent the rest of the day anticipating another suspicious Random Box, but one never came.

I only received a message from my neighbor that evening, "Did you send me a Random Box? It is the strangest thing. I can't seem to get rid of it."

The Demon of Tibbetts Hill

2004
Tibbitts Hill

"The cabin in the woods had been abandoned for years, but one night, a candle burned in the window," my uncle spoke in his theatric voice, holding a flashlight under his face.

The clock struck midnight, and I jerked forward, waking from my sleep on the couch.

"I had the craziest nightmare," I said, rubbing my eyes, trying to wake. I still felt anxious about my dream, but I couldn't remember why.

Another year, another reluctant family vacation. This year we are staying at a cabin in the woods of Tibbetts Hill, where my creepy uncle and his wife live.

My sister asked, "How would anyone even know a candle was burning one night if it was abandoned? Why do uncles always have the weirdest stories?"

She was bored, and with no phone signal in a four-person cabin sleeping six, she was in a very sour mood. She slung her legs over the armrest of the old chair she sat in and stared out the front door windows at the wind and rain we'd had all week.

"Are you kidding? Your uncle always tells the best scary stories; besides, scary stories don't always have to make sense. They're fun because they are spooky," defended our aunt as she snuggled up with her husband on the loveseat across from the couch. My mom smiled and lit a few candles on the coffee table, which I assumed was to help set the mood for the late-night story.

"We've already heard this one—the girl who didn't want to pick up the phone or something. Yes, yes, very scary," my sister casually dismissed as she played a game on her phone, still staring out the windows at the lightning striking in the distance.

Dad sat down on the couch beside me while disagreeing with my sister, "No, that one takes place in a haunted house, not a cabin. The cabin one is where two sailors are drinking whiskey, or swapping stories?"

My uncle appeared irritated but distracted by a tree fluttering in the window by increasing winds.

"Well, I haven't heard it," my mom said with anticipation, joining my dad and me on the couch. "I usually don't like scary stories, but I think it'll be fun with the rain and cozy blankets. Your uncle always scared me so much growing up."

She was always the one to see the best in an uncomfortable situation. My dad just rolled his eyes at my mom's excitement, making the rest of us laugh louder than the growing thunder we were trying to ignore.

"Thank you, but this story is one you haven't heard before. It takes place in these very woods. This story is about the demon of Tibbetts Hill, the Nagorath," My uncle turned off several lamps to cast more shadows upon his face.

My sister and I giggled out of nervousness.

"The cabin in the woods had been abandoned for years, but one night, a candle burned in the window. The townspeople nearby became scared. See, this cabin wasn't a normal cabin. No, a candle in the cabin's window meant the creature roamed the woods and warned the town to extinguish their lights. Even a single lit candle was enough to attract the demon, a creature of darkness that preyed on the light. Whoever lit the candle would be eaten as a sacrifice, appeasing the creature for a time."

We seemed frozen in time. Only the storm and the clock on the wall dared move as we listened intently to my uncle speak.

"They say the Nagorath is a demon without form with horrible power. In these woods, late at night, it will look for light to feed…."

"OooOOOooo," my dad said, mimicking a ghost. It broke up the moment's tension, and we all joked along.

The wind's howling grew outside, and what was once the sound of rain became a torrent of water. Just as my uncle was about to continue when the storm struck, turning off the power, and giving a jump.

"I'm sure it was just a fuse," my dad reassured with a chuckle in the dark, and he turned to find the fuse box. The rest of us groaned in disappointment.

"Great… now I can't even charge my useless phone," my sister complained.

My mom got up from the couch to find and hand out flashlights. My aunt walked around and lit a few more candles on the coffee table and windowsills to give the room a dim glow from their flames.

Everyone drew close to the center of the cabin. After a long, deep rumble of thunder, my uncle tried to reset himself, "Maybe I should start at the top? The cabin in the woods had been abandoned for years…."

My aunt encouragingly grabbed her husband's arm, "How many more times will we need to start the story over before we get on with it."

My uncle scoffed at his wife and distorted his face again with a flashlight in the dark. His voice became more focused and deliberate toward my sister and me, "The Nagorath brought living nightmares to anyone with light. The towns stayed in the dark, but decades passed, and eventually, the cabin became abandoned. Soon the memories turned to stories, and the cabin turned to rot."

My dad feigned a loud snore with his eyes closed that made the rest of us giggle, but our laughter was quickly replaced by another loud clap of thunder that made us all jump. My uncle smiled and continued, "But one night, someone lit the candle again in the old cabin. The townspeople who remembered the old tales tried to prepare, but it wasn't enough. People hid in cellars, closets, and churches, but it didn't matter. The Nagorath came anyway."

"But who tried to warn them?" My mom asked. I could see her hold my dad much tighter than earlier.

"Nobody knows," my uncle replied.

Loose tree branches flew through the forest, battering the cabin's outer walls and clawing at its windows. The storm's violent winds produced a sound of desperate moaning within the cacophony of the screaming gale.

My sister moved her legs off the chair's armrest and sat up to face my uncle, "What did the Nagorath do to the town?"

My uncle leaned in and spoke even slower, "This demon feeds on the fear in your soul, binding you in a moment in time to live an eternal nightmare. Over and over, sadistically reliving its attack, until it grows tired of your infinite pain and consumes you."

"That doesn't make any sense," my sister said in confusion.

"Wait, what? I don't get it," said my mom, who nudged my dad. "Do you get it?"

"Guys, it's really not that hard--," I began to explain.

The front door blew off the hinges as a creature burst into the cabin. While wooden debris peppered my parents as they dove away from the blown open entrance. I screamed as the door landed, pinning me down on the couch.

Making its way to the center of the cabin, it was a form beyond any adequate description I could give. It had teeth where eyes should be and mucus where there should be skin. Antlers of a mighty buck pierced through its veil of pallid moist flesh as a tangled nest of tentacles propelled its form underneath. Its exterior dissolved and reformed, oscillating its very shape and countenance.

Everyone dropped their flashlights, and all but a single candle blew out, making what I saw even more difficult to believe. Mom cowered on the floor before the kaleidoscopic terror, shuddering with terror as the creature lurched closer. The monstrosity unhinged a jaw of a thousand teeth and swallowed her whole. Her muffled screaming lasted only a moment within the god-forsaken creature.

A long tentacle caught and dangled my dad in the air before dropping him into its gaping jaw. My aunt and uncle broke for the backdoor. Tentacles with small mouths formed from its side, latched onto my aunt and uncle, and ate them alive one mouthful at a time.

Once finished, the demon slowly moved toward where I lay still pinned onto the couch. Pelleted by the storm and traumatized by the being beyond.

I couldn't breathe. I couldn't move. I sniffled as tears ran down my cheek, silently anticipating whatever terrible fate this creature had prepared for me. Looking away, I tried to focus on the last remaining lit candle on the windowsill instead of the horror looming near.

The abomination slowly moved near my face, and long needles birthed from its ungodly form. I lay paralyzed as it penetrated my skin, which it greedily savored.

In my pain, all I could whimper was a small disintegrating prayer, "Oh my god."

Lips then split from a pustulous mound and uttered, "Even the gods have lost count of your horrors and have long since not cared. The cabin in the woods had been abandoned for years, but one night, a candle burned in the window."

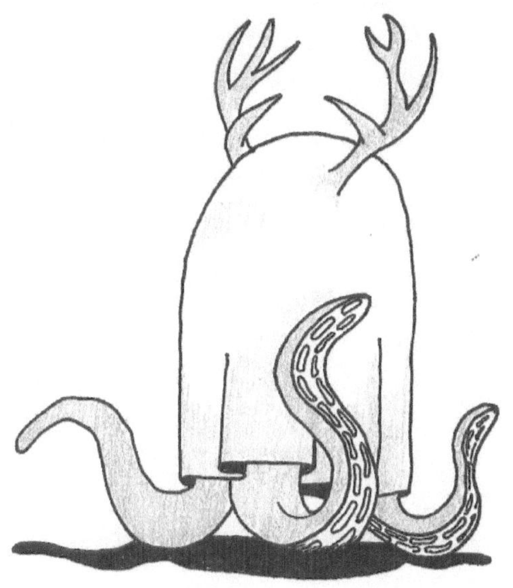

Figure 7.

The clock struck midnight, and I jerked forward, waking from my sleep on the couch.

"I had the craziest nightmare," I said, rubbing my eyes, trying to wake. I still felt anxious about my dream, but I couldn't remember why.

A Gossip of Mermaids

1703
Rye, NH

"I had worked aboard his ship, the *Hades*, for six years and then became a free man again," Isaac Freeman told me as I bought him another round of whiskey.

The *Purple Clam* was like any other bar in Rye, except this bar didn't care who its patrons were. This bar had Isaac Freeman, the former indentured servant to Mr. Penny, the former fleet manager of the Tamberlane Supply Company.

Isaac kept folding a small book again and again in his hand as he recounted his story to me.

"I was born a free man, but freedom isn't free. I left my wife and newborn in Virginia to work in Rye. My servitude in exchange for my family's financial debt. I was only away for three months when I received word my little boy, Rael, died of infection. I couldn't even go to the funeral. Then two months later, my wife left me for a new life with the money meant to pay off the debt."

"Marden's Cove. Tell me about Marden's Cove," I impatiently instructed. I could barely contain my excitement. His rambling was of no use to me. "A rumor says you've been. Have you seen the wealth beyond measure stored there?"

"Oh, Marden's Cove? Mr. Penny offered me a double portion to lead him into Marden's Cove. I told him to commute the rest of my contract. He obliged, and we headed down to the cove that night. See, Mr. Penny had heard from the other sailors that the cook went to the cove on a drunken night to wish that he could leave his servitude, and then he never returned. Mr. Penny didn't care about the cook. He just believed the damned fool of a story," Isaac said, then polished off his glass, tapping its side for another.

I shook my head no and prepared to leave the filthy bar and Isaac Freeman when he grabbed the edge of my coat and tugged me back toward my stool.

"A child's story calls it the *Well of Dreams*—a place where a gossip of mermaids make wonders come true to those who shout their wishes inside. Of course, the odor pushes away most visitors, and the lack of wildlife and fish keep hunters and fishermen away. That's not a place to visit. This is a cove you die in."

"You didn't go to Marden's Cove?" I asked.

"I said I did because I did. The cove's entrance is down in a steep ravine of jagged rocks jetting through the water. The wind over the rocks almost sounded like whistling. It is a tight winding crack in the land. People can get stuck, wedged in by the tide, and drown."

I sat back down. Wanting to hear more, I ordered him another round. He must be giving me caution for a reason.

Isaac continued, "Mr. Penny shouted into the cave, 'I want wealth beyond measure.' I told him we needed to go deeper to see the well. The further we went, the narrower the walls became. He kept shouting and demanding they give him wealth and power."

I began to wonder where Isaac Freeman was heading with this.

"We reached a wide opening where a small well was constructed, the Well of Dreams. Mr. Penny shouted again and again into it, becoming furious that no mermaids had appeared. I suggested we turn back as the tide started to roll in. Then just like that," Isaac Freeman snapped his fingers. "A mermaid appeared in the well. She was beautiful and surreal with long flowing dark hair. She motioned him over, whispered something in his ear, and dragged him down deep in the well."

Figure 8.

My eyes were glued to the former indentured servant, who finished his glass of whisky.

"When I looked into the well to see where he went, another mermaid appeared. As beautiful as the last, with dark skin like mine. I shouted that I wished for a new life!" Isaac Freeman then leaned in close to me. "She said to me, 'The gods have lost count of your horrors and have long since not cared. Come with me, and I will show you a life where you can start again.' She brought my head close to hers. I felt my mind in a trance as I leaned in and kissed her. I felt her arms wrap around me and drag me into the waters."

Isaac raised his hands in the air and then threw them down beneath the bar height in a dramatic fashion.

"The next thing I knew, I had washed ashore on the beaches of Rye. All I had in my possession was this little black book, my signed certificate, and the fleet manager's purse. Ensuring my freedom," said Isaac Freeman with a smug smile.

"So the mermaids must've answered his wish, just like they answered yours?" I was euphoric in my joy. "I will pay you handsomely. How much for you to lead me to Marden's Cove tonight?"

"I'll take whatever you have in your purse," Isaac smiled as I bought him another round of whiskey.

Prayer, Radio, and the Calling

April 1945
Southwestern Germany
B-17 "*The Jezebel Spirit*"

"The sea gave up their dead, judged according to their books, and cast into the lake of fire."

"Way to set the mood, Evans," Captain Sanders interrupted. Pilot Evans put down his miniature bible and was about to reply when Sanders cut him off. "You ever wonder why God doesn't just stop the war, or do you even think he cares?"

"The Lord works in mysterious ways, my friend," replied Evans.

"Truth is in simplicity, not confusion," radio operator Hanson said.

Sanders chucked in response, looking back at Hanson over the bomb bay's narrow catwalk from the pilot's cabin.

Hanson inquired over the radio, "I still don't know how the Germans could've gotten in behind us like that. We've already taken Riegelsberg, and the Nazis are retreating to Berlin. The flimsy didn't say anything new about a German front. Why all the secrecy? Why all the rush? They got us birds loaded in ridiculous cloud cover with a crumby mickey unit for radar. We barely had time to refuel, and we still need repairs."

"Our *Jezebel Spirit* will hold together. We know our targeted location; we just have to seek it out and deliver the payload," reminded Sanders.

"But what is 'It'?" Hanson asked but couldn't be heard over the static interference.

Figure 9.

"The Lord is on our side. By his tender mercy alone, we will return in one piece if we believe in him," Evans said, kissing his miniature bible and then holding it to his chest.

"Nice sermon, Reverend," Sanders remarked, then cleared his throat. "I got one for ya. Grovel, for we are but the grain of the fields. Ready to be hewn down and consumed."

"I am not familiar with that verse. What book is that?" Asked Evans with a disgusted face.

"It's from a much older prophet. One they don't talk about at Sunday school," Sanders snickered, waving a small black book about the same size as Evans' bible. Evans sneered at the Captain, who laughed for uncomfortably too long after his own remark.

Rumors claimed Captain Sanders was a strange man who spoke with demons and searched for occult items beyond the German lines. Hanson asked him, "Where did you get that book anyways?"

"This was one of the few copies that survived the Rye Harbor book burning of 1912. Can't read most of it, but what I can read... It offers me an awakening. It calls out to me."

"The *Jezebel Spirit* is kept in the sky with science, and by science alone, we communicate. Not through prayer or a calling," Hanson said, waving the microphone in the direction of the pilots.

"Oh yeah?" Sanders refuted through the radio's heavy static. "How's our signal?"

In defeat, Hanson turned back to his table and adjusted several of the dials, "Radio is still patchy. We left before we could receive the needed parts. We receive signals easily enough, but with its busted unit, anyone likely will miss a message unless we repeat it a lot."

"It's important not to give up hope. 'Thine eyes shall see the king in his beauty: they shall behold the land that is very far off.'

Holding onto the light is the only option," Evans replied, waving his scripture again.

"There is no way it should be this quiet," Sanders remarked, now disinterested in the conversation. Sanders fidgeted in his seat as much as the engine rattled the plane. He seemed unnerved and distressed as he squirmed in discomfort. He quickly removed his headset before panicking at the helm, "Did you see that?!"

"See what?" Evans asked in anxious confusion.

"What is that thing? A face in the clouds!" Sanders began screaming, hitting the control panel, and throwing the yoke left and right, crying out, "Every man to their stations, get those bombs ready to drop. Go, Go, Go!"

"Hanson, radio the *Essex*. We are about to collide!" Evans cried as he fought his co-piolet. Evans shouted with fright as he looked at Sanders, "Sanders, your eyes. Your black eyes!"

At that moment, the craft shook, causing all on *the Jezebel Spirit* to jostle in the significant turbulence. A hole was torn open in the side of the plane from colliding with another aircraft. Waves of fire rolled in, and the open cabin air ripped several other crew members out. Weightless in their spiraled descent, the crew that remained were baptized in waves of fire and smoke. Hanson was dislodged from his chair and hurled into a pile of parachutes and supplies.

The flying fortress unceremoniously forced landed into an embankment before sliding into a canal, covering the bomber with debris and water.

Hanson woke to the pitch-black interior of the plane, miraculously finding a working flashlight next to him. He made his way from the back of the aircraft to the pilot's cabin. He found his friends mutilated, torn, and crushed beneath the debris—Captain Evans was missing an arm, and Sanders's neck snapped and was missing his eyes. Hanson patted them down to take their dog tags, curiously only finding a gold medallion on Sanders.

Unable to open a panel to leave, Hanson panicked and held his head for a moment to think before looking for the radio. Once found, it still managed to be turned on. Hopeful, he stripped the wires on the broken headphones and roughly twisted them back together with the broken line on the receiver.

"Please, please, please, please," Hanson said to himself as he made some quick repairs. After a few adjustments, he could hear a signal through the static.

"Eureka!" Hanson huffed as sounds began to come through the speaker. All he could make it out was:

> "…*The awakening is coming...*"

The radio offered just the one transmission before going silent and dying.

In anger, Hanson slammed on the radio. No sooner had Hanson moved that water started to flow into the compartment from the canal. He could feel the shift of the plane as the wreckage started to slide into the water. The undelivered bomb payload began to press and screech against one another in the drowning plane.

In desperation, Hanson got on his knees in the growing muddy water and prayed, "God, save me. Let me see home again."

Hanson cried to his prayer.

As the cold river water came just over the legs of the knelt radio operator, Sanders' small black book floated up in the water in front of Hanson.

Hanson opened the small book and flipped past drawings of madness to pages of ugly and unpronounceable words smudged by blood and mud. Hanson read a small legible portion aloud, "When the stars will be stripped away, and the ruler of this outer darkness will ride beneath the waters. Great houses will emerge from the depths and come for the souls that cry."

Hanson's eyes became weary. The waters rose, the dirt slid, and the bombs' shells clanged under the plane's moving weight. The metal shells screeched and jolted until one collapsed onto his leg, pinning him down. Hanson cried out in agony, and as he lay there, he held Sanders' gold medallion tightly as he wept in the muddy wreckage.

After a single flickering light, somehow, the radio turned on again.

Hanson reached for the receiver, unsure if anyone would hear him, and frantically cried, "Please, I am trapped. If you can hear me, help me. Anybody. I'll do anything. Hear the sound of my voice. I am trapped. I repeat.

"Please, I am trapped. If you can hear me, help me. Anybody. I'll do anything. Hear the sound of my voice. I am trapped. I repeat.

"Please, I am trapped. If you can hear me, help me. Anybody. I'll do anything. Hear the sound of my voice. I am trapped. I repeat…"

And all radio operator Hanson thought of as he repeated was to not give up hope,

…forever.

<u>Richard Penny</u>

February 2014
Palm Beach, FL

Palm Beach can be warm in February, but it wasn't today. Overcast and cold rain brought a chilly morning to South Florida. I never thought the low 50's looked good on palm trees, and certainly not how I envisioned retirement.

My old friend Poppy insisted on brunch at *Le Bilboquet*. I decided to travel light that gloomy morning, bringing only my phone, wallet, and keys stuffed in my old wet jacket. The rain came to an immediate halt once I arrived at the restaurant. Surprisingly, the *Le Bilboquet* was empty.

My phone notified me of Poppy's messages:

> *Something came up*
>
> *Don't go to Bilboquet today*
>
> *Sorry*

I had looked forward to eating, but with the clouds departing, I realized I hadn't seen the beach in some time and wanted to watch the waves while I had a few minutes of sunlight.

As I made my way to the shore, I saw a short bald man place traffic cones blocking direct access to the beach.

"I'll make my way down Hammon," I thought.

Turning the corner, I felt the first warmth all morning. The sun's rays were beaming straight down at me, just over the pink *Colony Hotel*.

A loud '*thwap*' startled me. I turned to where the sound came from to see a little black book lying on the ground from several feet away.

There was a name printed on its front:

Richard Penny

I bent down and picked up the wet book. When I flipped through the pages filled with strange drawings and notes, some I could read, and others I couldn't.

"An artist, maybe," I thought to myself. "Or maybe an author?"

I looked around to see who this could've belonged to— Nearby, a man wearing an 'Econo-Gas' hat was staring at his phone.

"I think you dropped something," I insisted, holding the small book out to him.

He seemed not to notice what I said and walked away into the nearby hotel. Seeing no one else, I followed him to the entrance only to find the door locked.

"Odd for a hotel to lock its front door," I thought, but I knocked to get someone's attention. The door cracked open, and a single eye glared through the slit at me.

Caught off-guard at first from the gazing eye, I managed to utter, "Um, hello, is a Richard Penny staying here? I believe he dropped this book."

The door opened completely, and the concierge allowed me in, motioning me to follow him through the foyer of the chicly pink hotel.

"*Le Bilboquet* isn't the only place empty today," I thought as we walked through its vacant halls.

Before I could explain, the concierge motioned me into a guestroom where a woman stood beside an empty chair. He shoved me in and closed the door behind me, making me extremely nervous.

She looked at me, lit cigarette in hand, analyzing me up and down.

Confused, I offered the little black book to her, "This is for Richard Penny?"

The woman took a long drag and shook her head, disgusted at my wet attire. She gestured I take a seat. I was confused but obliged, and then she handed me a bag. I opened it to find two large bands of cash, each with a note of ten thousand dollars.

My heart raced. I opened my mouth to resist or ease my confusion, but the woman silently insisted I follow her as she walked out the door.

"I don't know what game this is, but I just…." I began to say, but I could not focus. I didn't know if I was moving slowly or if she was walking fast, but I had to chase her down the hall into another room.

As I entered, the woman pressed me against a wall. She took several steps back next to a short bald man with a large camera in his hands and took another drag of her cigarette.

I asked the short bald man, "Richard Penny?"

The man held up the camera and replied, "Yes. Hello Richard. Smile."

I grimaced. Then a flash and a moment later, I had my face on a passport printed out with the name 'Richard Penny.'

"No. I am not Richard Penny," I rebuffed in confusion.

The door to the room creaked open, and a designer wheeled in a cart filled with clothes.

"Richard Penny?" They asked. I raised my hand in surprise to myself, then awkwardly put it back down as the designer pushed the cart toward me.

"I'm looking for Richard Penny," I said as they helped me remove my jacket and bent down to get my measurements.

They retrieved a pair of white wool pants from the rack and instructed me to change.

"Change now?" I asked.

I was met with only a silent nod as they searched for a shirt. I even surprised myself when I began changing with each new piece of clothing they handed me.

Now dry and comfortable in my new suit, the short bald man opened the door for me to follow through.

I anxiously followed him and the woman back to the foyer and out to a long black car. Opening the door for us, I smiled back at the familiar-looking driver who wore an Econo-Gas hat.

"Richard Penny," acknowledged the driver as I made myself comfortable in the limo seat.

In the car, I was asked by the woman, "Richard Penny?"

"Yes?" I responded, knowing that wasn't my name.

She handed me a boarding pass.

Destination: Paris, France.

"Wonder what's next?" I asked myself.

The bald man handed me a jacket with a designer wallet in its breast pocket. I filled the wallet with the cash and put the book in my pocket.

My phone started buzzing with a text from Poppy:

Please call me

Something weird is happening

The woman showed me a new phone, which only a "Richard Penny" could have. As I took the new phone, the woman kept her hand out, reaching for my old one. The woman smiled as I handed it to her in disgust.

Poppy would need to wait.

I hardly realized that the car had stopped at the airport while still admiring my sleek new phone. I stepped out, expecting the bald man and woman to follow, but they closed the door behind me, and the car hurried off.

I checked the gate number and made my way through the airport, looking for the terminal. I could see a private jet docked and ready for me.

"Name, please," The ticket agent requested.

"Richard Penny," I responded. After showing my passport and pass, they permitted me through.

As I boarded the jet, I mused, "Again, empty."

After several minutes of waiting and no one else boarding. Several agents entered the cabin with 'FBI' on their jackets.

"Richard Penny?" They asked me with a stern, commanding tone.

"No, no, I…." I trailed, thinking of my new ID. I checked for my phone, only to realize my face was on the new phone's background.

"Richard Penny?" They approached further still, hands-on their holsters.

I thought back to the small black book I first found. Frantic, I pulled it from my pocket and ruffled through pages of strange words and drawings; as receipts from *Le Bilboquet* and the *Colony Hotel* fell from the book's pages.

"Richard Penny?! Hands in the air!" The agents shouted, now with weapons drawn. Breathing heavily, I screamed inside in panic and confusion, dropping the little black book.

"Richard Penny?!" They said.

"Richard Penny?" They said.

"Richard Penny."

Government Lethal Chambers

1920
Washington Square, NY

In response to the great book burning of 1912, New York opened its first legalized assisted suicide center.

The unknown manner in which the centers worked and the government's cold handling of them dissuaded fence-sitters. So when Nathanial crossed the road and walked down the short set of stairs into the lobby of the Government Lethal Chamber, it had been on his mind for days. Something about the morning's bitter winds helped him work up the nerve to end it all.

The lobby was empty. The only things in it were a dozen cheap folding chairs against the wall and a receptionist's desk. Its off-white tile floor and beige walls did nothing to sway his mind, but he was sure that was its intention. Nathanial figured it wasn't the place that needed to worry about comfort.

After a moment of standing alone, a nurse walked out of the service door and sat behind the desk. Her smile was calm and welcoming beneath her sad eyes.

"Welcome," she said. She brought a thick stack of papers on a clipboard and handed Nathanial a cheap ballpoint pen. "Let me know if you have any questions."

Nathanial smiled insincerely back and looked down at the heavy stack of paperwork. It must've been a hundred pages. He supposed there wasn't any reason to have a lengthy discussion. They both knew why he was there. The nurse had even been kind enough to highlight all the parts he needed to sign and initial.

The nurse grabbed several forms behind the desk and disappeared back through the doors deeper into the facility.

The more he signed, the heavier the clipboard seemed to become, and even before even halfway through his forms, the pen began to dry. Nathanial rolled the tip of the ballpoint pen furiously to try and dispel some ink. His frustration was only distracted by the sound of the front door opening. Walking in was a woman wearing a large hat that blocked a view of her face.

Nathanial tried not to stare, but she stood out, being the only other person in the room.

The woman made herself comfortable as she sat opposite him and placed her hat on an adjacent chair. Nathanial found her very attractive, but he had never been good with women. Several times he tried to work up the nerve to make eye contact or speak, but each time he evaded just as her eyes started to look his way.

Eventually, the nurse came back out through the doors. She grabbed another stack of forms from behind the desk and approached the woman. Nathanial couldn't hear what they were saying but could see the nurse handing the woman the clipboard with paper and a cheap pen before disappearing into the back again.

Time seemed to stretch out into eternity.

Nathanial became frustrated with every line as the ink from his pen reluctantly trickled out. Digging harder into the paper each time, he wrote his name. Every letter became more difficult than the one before. He looked back over to the woman, who had signed a dozen more pages.

Nathanial hoped that maybe she would look again at him just once more. Each time looking only to be disappointed, he would return to trying to sign his own forms.

After several more minutes, he heard the woman set the clipboard down on the chair beside her with the pen resting on top.

After one more feeble attempt to get the pen working, he worked up the courage to approach the woman. The clipboard shook in his hands as Nathanial walked over and asked, "I'm so sorry, but I believe my pen has died. Could I use yours?"

"That's not the only thing dying in here," the woman replied.

Nathanial was shocked by the dark humor, but he couldn't help but laugh.

The woman also busted out a short laugh and handed Nathanial her pen.

They made eye contact, and he realized she had the most beautiful brown eyes and rich dark hair. He stared into her eyes until she asked with a sad smile, "What?"

"Nothing. I just wouldn't have guessed that someone as beautiful as you would be here in a place like this."

Her eyes started to water up, "Well, it just seemed like the best option. I'm guessing you thought that, too, right? That's why you need the pen?"

Nathanial looked down at the clipboard and his new pen, "I guess you're right."

He gave her a quick smile and sat several chairs away. Nathanial turned his body away from her direction, assuming he had bothered her, and resumed filling out his forms.

Several pages later, he heard a wrapper crinkle and saw the woman open up a half-eaten muffin. Slowly enjoying several bites and then she finished the pastry.

"You know I'm going to miss Nathan's muffins. I figured I'd make it the last thing I tasted. You know, just in case this isn't the end, and the last thing I taste is my only experience after this. It's silly, I know," she said before wadding up the last couple of crumbs and placing them in her mouth.

"I used to work there. Actually, I used to own it. I'm Nathanial, by the way. Former owner of Nathan's Bakery."

"Oh, wow! I love your muffins."

Nathanial looked ashamed, "Once I was forced to sell it, the new owners they, um, ship in the muffins in now. They get them off the back of a Tamberlane truck. We don't make them anymore."

The woman gave an awkward half-smile and looked down at the floor.

"I don't think I'll miss anything. I'm not getting any better. The drugs aren't helping, and the doctor's bills keep rising. I can't keep up with that," Nathanial gruffed as his shaking hands bent and pulled his stack of papers, sniffling as he slammed it back onto his lap.

"I'm sorry," said the woman with an emphatic tone.

"You know, I just never caught a break. I'd make it to the top. They'd all see what I could do. I…," Nathanial stopped, whipped his nose on his sleeve, and looked back at the woman whose eyes were full of pity. He concluded with a simple, "Sorry."

Nathanial went back to filling out the forms.

The woman hid her face in her hands and began to cry. Nathanial silently looked on as she wallowed in her grief.

"My mum died last week. She was the only person who really understood me."

"Well, maybe, there is someone else who could understand…," Nathanial began to say.

"The cancer returned, and my mum was the one person with me every step of the way. I just don't have the strength to fight it again," she continued to cry.

Nathanial closed his mouth and returned to his paperwork, nearing the end.

Figure 10.

"Why don't cannibals eat clowns? Because they taste funny", the woman sniffled and giggled out her joke. Freeing a napkin from her purse, she wiped her nose, still giggling. "I just want to remember the jokes my mum always used to say. She was hilarious."

Nathanial smiled at her, content that she didn't seem to hate him. He looked back at the forms and finished another page.

"There's really nothing you'll miss?" The woman asked.

Nathanial stopped writing, unsure how to answer the question and puzzled as to why she'd still talk to him.

"You don't even have a favorite book or person?" The woman prodded.

Nathanial sat in silence as he thought, "I had some unfinished business, but I think it'll just need to stay that way, I'm afraid. Won't take long for others to move on."

Nathanial knew everything he was trying to say was wrong and looked at his paperwork more intensely.

"You think this is it? That this is the end?"

"I hope it is," Nathanial let slip out.

"I hope I see my mum again. I guess I won't know if that doesn't turn out to be true, but just to have one more breakfast with her would mean everything to me. She loved the bakery. Going there now, I'm just surrounded by strangers. Hundreds of people around me, talking, and no one knows me."

Nathanial tried to think of something to reciprocate but couldn't think of a single thing to say.

"I think you're beautiful," Nathanial finally said.

The woman smiled at him, then motioned him to come closer, "You want to hear another one of my mum's favorite jokes?"

Nathanial's eyes started to well up, hearing her sweet voice continue to talk to him. He didn't say a word and just nodded.

"Why did the chicken cross the road?"

Nathanial was confused and just shook his head.

"To get to the other side."

Nathanial gave a short snort of a laugh, and the woman laughed as well.

The nurse walked back through the doors and approached the woman. She quietly picked up the woman's completed paperwork and briskly looked through them.

"Please follow me," the nurse said and headed back toward the service door.

The woman took a deep breath, stood up, and walked behind the nurse.

She was only a few steps away when Nathanial dropped to his knees on the floor. His eyes welled up as he pleaded, "Please kiss me. Let my last memory be your lips."

The woman turned back to him with a sad sigh, "I can't have my last memory be a stranger's."

She turned and followed the nurse through the chamber doors.

He stayed on the ground a moment longer before standing up and returning to the chair beside her abandoned hat. Nathanial collected his pen and clipboard and picked up where he left off. Signing and initialing as he went, making sure not to leave tears where he signed.

As Nathanial wrote his name across the final line, the nurse walked back through the door,

"Nathanial, it's your time."

Quantum State of Love

1979
Tibbitts Hill

New England leaves swept up into crisp autumn air as the moving truck sped down the road.

Doug's parents moved to a small town in the countryside for his dad's new job at Tamberlane Supply, the regional supply distributor. Which meant new friends at a new school. The house next door had a daughter about his age named Patty. A beautiful girl with dark brown hair and a friendly smile. She only had to wave at him for him to know it was true love. She invited him over to play and did so every day after until the first day of fifth grade when they walked into the school hand in hand. She made him forget about where he was headed, and he didn't really care as long as it was with her.

People would say that young love doesn't last, but schoolyard kisses turned into high school affection. From school work and sports to prom dresses and parties, senior year came and went in a blink of an eye. The world of college lay before them, which led to fewer visits, fewer phone calls, and dating others.

Finding the courage to live his own life. Doug left town, chartered his own course, and made his own memories. Navigating through a tumultuous life of excess and loss.

Doug traveled the world, becoming lost in its wonderment and hopeless in its indifference. But no matter where he wandered, his mind always drifted back to Patty. The loudest parties didn't have her smile, and his loneliest darkness didn't have her touch.

He ultimately settled in a small home not far from where he grew up. He got a stable job at Tamberlane Supply and did his best every day.

Years passed, and contact with Patty became far less frequent. He heard she married a wealthy man and always appeared to be happy. He didn't dare reach out. Even if he'd had the nerve, he wouldn't have known what to say.

Every year he wanted to apologize but didn't know what about.

Every year he wanted to fix something that didn't seem broken.

Every year he felt a little sadder but couldn't remember why.

Every year he wished, deep down, that it would all just be over.

Doug had days he wished he would turn around and see ghosts. Just so he would know he wasn't alone, or at least that the memories were real.

He spent his remaining working years never getting a promotion at Tamberlane Supply before retiring at age seventy-five after a stroke.

He had a couple more years left in him before his eyes rolled back and exhausted his last breath. There was no pain, just a black wave of death rolling over him, sailing him into a tranquil release of the world and the life that he had known. Memories of all he had loved and feared began to dissipate in his last fleeting moments of life, and his consciousness drifted into the aether.

A dense, bright light flooded his mind, and an eternity of distant white encapsulated him.

Figure 11.

2038
Tibbitts Hill

Doug lifted off his Tamberlane virtual reality headset and put it beside him on the couch, then shook his head to get his bearing back. He looked over at his wife Patty, who had woken up from her session just a moment before.

"You didn't choose me?" Doug asked with an indignant tone.

Patty ignored him while she put her hair in a bun before offering an annoyed sigh of the obligation to answer his question.

"Ya, that's bound to happen, sweetheart. Remember last month when you didn't even want to date me because I worked at a gas station? It's not always going to be perfect, but we still had a fun time together, right? I'll tell you what. We'll do another session tonight, and I'm sure this time we'll be together again, okay? Now I have to meet up with Carroll at the *Purple Clam*."

Patty grabbed her purse and started for the door. Turning back to her husband just before she opened the door, she said, "In this lifetime, I had three guys hold onto lifelong obsessions with me. Sometimes, while you're in it, it's hard to remember that it's all just a game."

Doug Sampson sat up and tried to wrap his mind around what he had endured.

www.ingramcontent.com/pod-product-compliance
Lightning Source LLC
Chambersburg PA
CBHW031549310726
48971CB00008B/2686